COLOUR JETS

Cosmic Kev

Andrew Donkin
and Jeff Cummins

Collins

COLOUR JETS

With much love for Sheila Brand – for grace under fire.

First published in paperback in Great Britain
by HarperCollins Publishers Ltd 1998

The HarperCollins website address is
www.**fire**and**water**.com

10 9 8 7 6 5 4 3 2

Text © Andrew Donkin 1999
Illustrations © Jeff Cummins 1999

The author and illustrator assert the moral right to be
identified as the author and illustrator of the work.

A CIP record for this title is available from the British Library.

ISBN 0 00 675381 7

Printed in Hong Kong.

Chapter 1

It had all gone horribly, horribly wrong. Kevin should never have opened his big,

He should never have said *anything*.

That night, Kevin decided he'd had enough of being laughed at. If there was one UFO, there had to be others. He'd spot another and shut everyone up.

They never have to wait this long on *The X Files*.

However, thick grey clouds filled the night sky. After an hour of gazing at nothing, Kevin gave up.

He wondered if there was another way of making contact. Perhaps aliens were telepathic. What if he concentrated really hard?

He did.

As Kevin went downstairs to hunt for some chocolate biscuits to boost his brainwaves, he caught sight of a light in the front garden.

I did it!

A light that shouldn't have been there.
It was **them!**

Chapter 2

Kevin's mind had reached across the
galactic wastes and the aliens had

I am Kevin
of Earth.

It was amazing.
It was fantastic.
  It wasn't going to last.

Then Kevin heard the sound of laughter and the light suddenly went out.

Tomorrow morning at school, Kevin's humiliation would be complete.

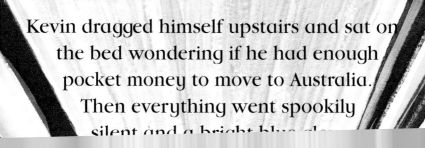

Kevin dragged himself upstairs and sat on
the bed wondering if he had enough
pocket money to move to Australia.
Then everything went spookily
silent and a bright blue glo...

He reached out and opened it.

Inside the wardrobe were several spiral galaxies, a huge red star, a rocket and some silver robot-things.

Chapter 3

The beings had opened an inter-
dimensional gateway into Kevin's

They were called Technobots and they
wanted Kevin to go with them.

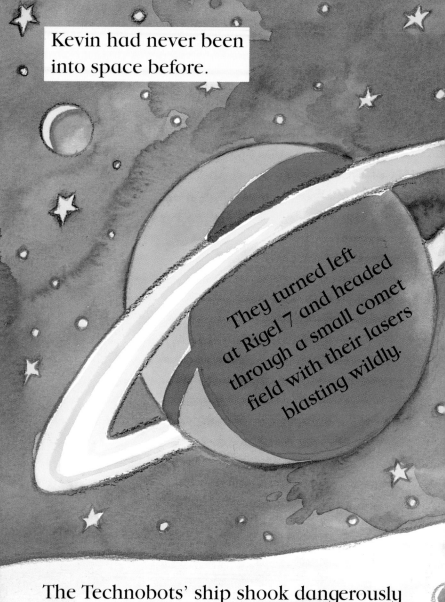

Kevin had never been into space before.

They turned left at Rigel 7 and headed through a small comet field with their lasers blasting wildly.

The Technobots' ship shook dangerously as it hurtled across the galactic wastes…

They were careful to avoid the dreaded Black ... Mizar

and headed into the Trifid Nebula.

Kevin watched as trails of space dust drifted past like cosmic candy floss.

15

Then the Technobots handed Kevin a white lab coat and a pair of glasses. (They had seen television programmes from Earth and knew what *real* scientists looked like.)

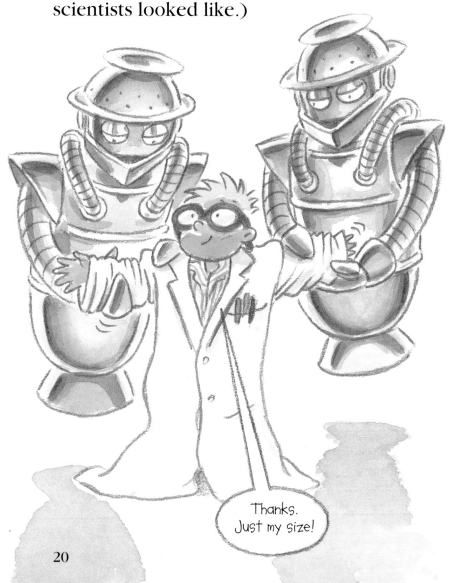

Kevin smiled weakly
and they left him to get on with it.

Chapter 4

Kevin studied the control panel of the Great Thinking Machine. Then he pressed the biggest button he could see.

Nothing happened.

He pressed another...

and another...

and another...

...until his hands become a blur.

and another...

Absolutely nothing happened.

Maybe there's a loose connection...?

Still nothing happened.

23

Nothing continued to happen for the next hour. Eventually, Kevin heard the Technobots coming back. Feeling very depressed, he looked for somewhere to hide. There was a space behind the machine, so Kevin crawled in.

Of course, in his heart of hearts, Kevin knew it couldn't be that simple.

But it was!

Kevin was a HERO!

He really enjoyed
the parade.

And the official party.

(But he wasn't too keen on the food.)

As Kevin signed autographs, he noticed
some of the Technobots whispering.
He asked them about going home.

The Technobots took him back to the
underground lab and locked him in.
That night he slept on a hard metal floor
and dreamt about eating chocolate
biscuits straight from the fridge.

Chapter 5

Next morning, Kevin was woken by strange sounds. A multi-limbed, automatic cleaning machine was busy sucking up dust and polishing everything in sight.

BEEP!
BEEP!

Suddenly, two shivers raced each other down Kevin's spine.

footst... a menacing figure loomed into the room.

Then the creature
broke into a huge grin
and said, "Hey! I'm Lloyd.
You're new round here, aren't you?"

Kevin explained his whole sorry story.
The scaly skin on Lloyd's forehead
rippled with horror
as he listened.

Typical! I hate it
when big people bully little
people just because
they can.

Lloyd told Kevin that the Technobots
couldn't do anything for themselves.
They'd stolen everything on their planet
from all over the universe – and now
they'd stolen Kev too!

"Will you help me?" asked Kevin. "Please."

"I'm just the cleaner," shrugged Lloyd.

Kevin scowled as the auto-cleaners scurried about. "I bet one of those stupid things unplugged the Great Thinking Machine," he thought.

"*Don't fall in by accident*," Kevin fumed, replaying Lloyd's words in his mind. "Ha! How stupid does he think I am?"

Then Kev's brain did a little sideways flip and suddenly he got it!

One 'accidental'
fall later...

All clean

Goodly good.

He had to share the tank with half a
tonne of very smelly rubbish, three Zass
dirt snakes (dead) and a Regillian sewer
rat (very much alive).

But Kevin didn't care. He was free!

After lunch they visited
Ceylon 7 where Lloyd
had a contract to
clean a giant
black monolith.

We're lucky today – sometimes it hums.

The most important job of the day was
the Imperial Museum of Art on Zinbarr.

Kevin and Lloyd started work on the breakable exhibits, while the auto-cleaners did the rest.

friends.

Kev reached up very carefully…

ZZZAPP!

…just as it was blasted into a zillion and one pieces!

It was the Technobots, and they didn't look happy!

Movie and we toot!

Chapter 7

The Technobots were really mad at

Then the museum guard saw the
shattered work of art...

That did it. For the first time in the museum's long and distinguished history, there was a sudden outbreak of war.

Lloyd grabbed Kevin and they ran for their lives. They tried to lose themselves among the galleries and exhibits.

But the Technobots weren't going to give up that easily.

Kevin and Lloyd collided with a school party. At least that seemed to slow down the opposition for a while.

Quick! This way!

"If we can just get back to the space ship…" yelled Lloyd, ripping open a fire exit.

Lloyd just had time to say, "Oh no!" before the Technobots fired. A huge ball

Something rolled across the floor and bounced into Kev's lap with a horrible BONG! sound.

Chapter 8

Suddenly, Kevin heard a muffled voice coming from Lloyd's chest. It said, "Help, Kev! Let me out!" Then a flap opened and inside was…

Lennie!

"Lloyd was just a mechanical suit," he explained. "Come on, let's get out of here."

"It's mad! Crazy!! Insane!!!" they agreed.
The really bad news was that no one
had ever managed to escape. They were

Kevin sat down, depressed. Now he'd
never get back home. Ever.

Kevin looked around at all the crashed alien ships... and his brain did another sideways flip. Maybe *not one* of them was powerful enough, but how about *all* of them together??

You mean, join all the ships into one massive, hyper—spacecraft and blast our way free? Hmmm... *I* like it... *I* like it a lot.

And we can reprogramme the auto-cleaners to do the work. All the welding and stuff.

Now all Kevin had to do was persuade the others to help.

Chapter 10

Since Earth wasn't involved in any

OK, as long as I don't have to sit next to the Gobbites. They eat their own noses, you know.

#~=+*∧/??

Meep. Meep.

Even the Technobots agreed to help, and promised that they'd never chase Kevin again - if his idea worked.

Lloyd reprogrammed
the auto-cleaners and
set them to work

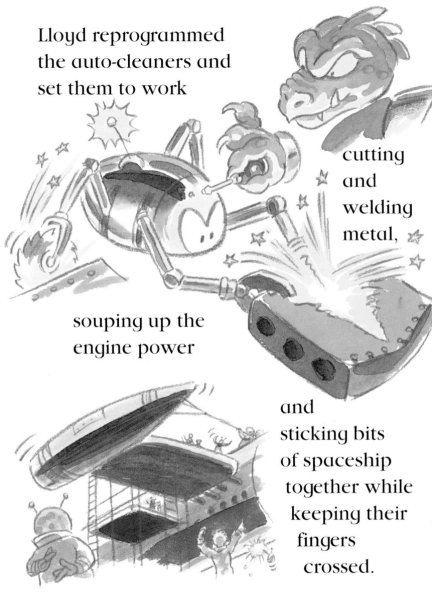

cutting
and
welding
metal,

souping up the
engine power

and
sticking bits
of spaceship
together while
keeping their
fingers
crossed.

Slowly (or perhaps quickly – no one
could really tell without clocks) the
hyper-spacecraft began to take shape.

58

Finally, the biggest, most colossal, gigantic, enormous, mammoth, most powerful, vast spaceship ever built anywhere in the

Everyone said very loudly that only Cosmic Kev could have pulled this off. (And everyone muttered quietly that it would all be his fault when it went wrong.)

Kevin and Lloyd climbed into the
command seats, and Kev started the
automatic countdown. All the aliens
with eyes shut them very tightly indeed.

10...   9...   8...

I wonder why no
one has ever tried
this before.

Who knows?
maybe we're the first
to think of it.

7... 6...

Maybe... but Kevin didn't think so.

Other people trapped in black holes must have tried this, but none of them had made it. Why not? At the very last

Kevin pressed 'reverse'.
The rocket's power imploded on itself and there was the most enormous BANG!

The stars went black and space became white. They reversed forwards (or went forwards in reverse) and blasted their way out of the black hole. All the aliens with mouths opened them very wide indeed and screamed at the top of their extraterrestrial voices.

Chapter 11

Cosmic Kev had done it again! He and
... all over the

They gave a little piece of the black
hole to the Zinbarr Imperial Museum,
to pay for the damage. No one had ever
escaped from a black hole before and it
soon became a big crowd-puller.

Now the Technobots had promised to leave him alone, Kevin could do anything he liked…

Look up old friends…

Pay Peter Barker a little visit…

Or even go into partnership with Lloyd and Lennie…

The only *real* problem was deciding what to do first!

THE COSMIC END